ALADDIN • An imprint of Simon & Schuster Children's Publishing Division • 1230 Avenue of the Americas, New York, New York 10020 • First Aladdin hardcover edition December 2020 • © 2020 Lisa Thiesing • Jacket illustration © 2020 Lisa Thiesing • All rights reserved, including the right of reproduction in whole or in part in any form • ALADDIN and related logo are registered trademarks of Simon & Schuster, Inc. • For information about special discounts for bulk purchases, please contact Simon & Schuster Special Sales at 1-866-506-1949 or business simonandschuster.com • The Simon & Schuster Speakers Bureau can bring authors to your live event. For more information or to book an event contact the Simon & Schuster Speakers Bureau at 1-866-248-3049 or visit our website at www.simonspeakers.com. • Book design by Karin Paprocki © 2020 by Simon & Schuster, Inc. • The illustrations for this book were rendered digitally. • The text of this book was set in Argentile. • Manufactured in China 1020 SCP • 2 4 6 8 10 9 7 5 3 1 • Library of Congress Control Number 2020938303 • ISBN 978-1-5344-6572-5 (hc) ISBN 978-1-5344-6573-2 (ebook)

A Friend Is . . .

LISA THIESING

Aladdin · NEW YORK · LONDON · TORONTO · SYDNEY · NEW DELHI

To all my friends…

with love

A friend is . . .
for making.

A friend is...

for skating

and for catching...

for singing,
singing,
singing...

and for giggling.

A friend is . . .

for listening,

sharing...

and for playing.

A friend is ...
for writing

and then for reading.

A friend is . . .

for reflecting . . .

for growing . . .

for hiding,

and for seeking.

A friend is . . .
for complaining,

appreciating...

and wondering.

A friend is ...

for jumping...

surprising . . .

and for giving.

A friend is . . .

forever.